This book belongs to:

To my lovely critique group, Candy and Mo, who believe in the power of storytelling.
Chitra

To my wonderful nephews Harry and Charlie Garratt.
Poonam

First published in the United Kingdom in 2018 by Lantana Publishing Ltd., London.
www.lantanapublishing.com

American edition published in 2018 by Lantana Publishing Ltd., UK.
info@lantanapublishing.com

Reprinted in 2018, 2019

Text © Chitra Soundar 2018
Illustration © Poonam Mistry 2018

Distributed in the United States and Canada by Lerner Publishing Group, Inc.
241 First Avenue North, Minneapolis, MN 55401 U.S.A.
For reading levels and more information, look for this title at www.lernerbooks.com
Cataloging-in-Publication Data Available.

Printed and bound in Europe.
Original artwork created with ink on paper and completed digitally.

ISBN: 978-1-911373-29-2
eBook ISBN: 978-1-911373-37-7

You're Safe With Me

Chitra Soundar

Poonam Mistry

LANTANA PUBLISHING

When the moon rose high and the stars twinkled, it was bedtime for baby animals. But that night, when the skies turned dark and the night grew stormy, the little ones couldn't sleep.

Mama Elephant was passing by. "Hush," she whispered, gently rocking the baby animals in her trunk.

"You're safe
with me."

SWISH-SWISH!
The trees moved.

OOH-OOH!
The wind moaned.

The little
animals
woke up and
whimpered.

"Don't worry about the wind,"
whispered Mama Elephant.

"He's an old friend of the forest.
He brings us seeds from faraway lands."

"He's loud,"
said little monkey.

"That's him huffing and
puffing because he's tired,"
said Mama Elephant. "He is as
gentle as a breeze when all the
work is done."

The baby animals closed
their eyes. The wind didn't
worry them anymore.

"You're safe with me,"
whispered Mama
Elephant.

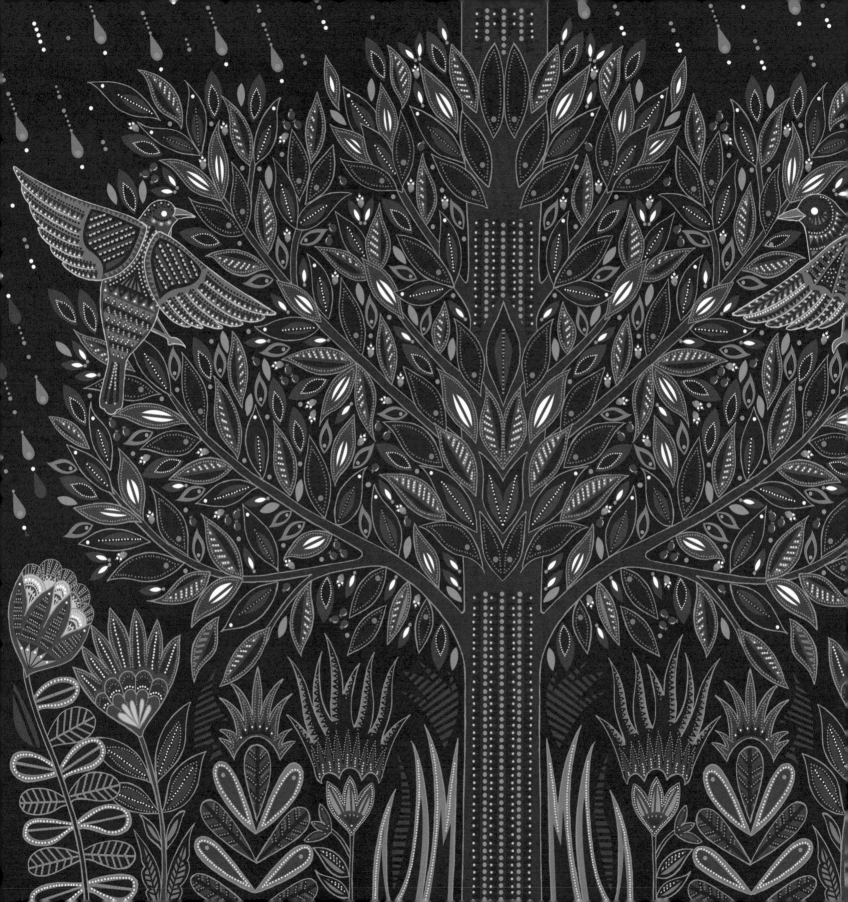

DUM-DE-DUM!
Thunder clattered.

DE-DUM, DE-DUM!
The clouds echoed.

The little animals
sat up startled.

"Don't be nervous," said Mama Elephant. "Thunder brings us water from the sea and makes this forest grow from scattered seeds."

"She's noisy,"
said little loris.

"She's groaning from the
weight of the rain," said
Mama Elephant. "Soon she
will turn as fluffy as cotton
flowers."

The little ones relaxed.
Thunder didn't terrify
them anymore.

"You're safe with me,"
whispered Mama
Elephant.

CRACK-TRACK!
The sky lit up.

FLASH-SNAP!
The night flickered.

The little animals
gasped.

"Don't be frightened,"

whispered Mama
Elephant.

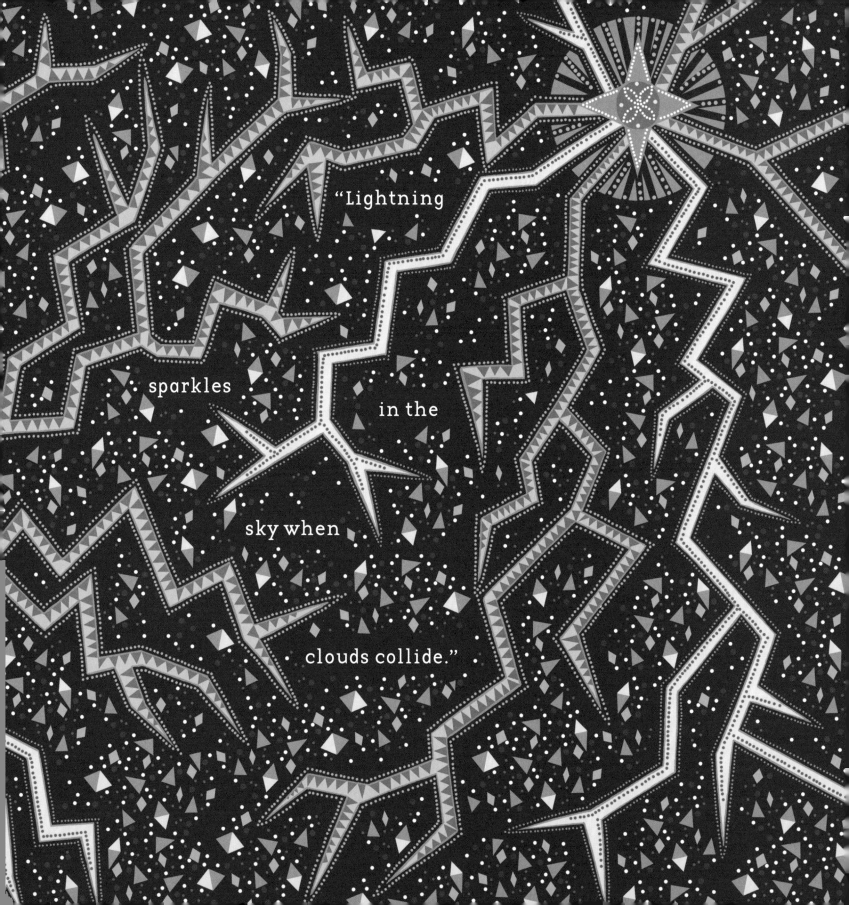

"Lightning

sparkles

in the

sky when

clouds collide."

"He's bright!" said
tiger cub.

"He turns into little
shiny stars when thunder
returns to the sea," said
Mama Elephant.

The baby animals relaxed
in Mama Elephant's hug.
Lightning didn't frighten
them anymore.

"You're safe with me,"
whispered Mama Elephant.

GURGLE-GURGLE!
The river rumbled.

RIBBIT-RIBBIT! The frogs croaked. The little ones trembled.

"Don't mind the river," whispered Mama Elephant. "She takes the water from the rain back to the sea, so the sea will never dry up."

"Is she angry?"
asked little pangolin.

"That's just her stomach
grumbling with hunger," said
Mama Elephant. "Soon she
will eat all the shadows in the
forest. When she finishes, it
will be morning again."

The little animals closed
their eyes. The river didn't
scare them anymore.

Slowly the little
ones fell asleep
as Mama Elephant
whispered, "You're
safe with me."